PAJ PLAYSCRIPT SERIES

General Editors: Bonnie Marranca and Gautam Dasgupta

OTHER TITLES IN THE SERIES:

THEATRE OF THE RIDICULOUS/Kenneth Bernard, Charles Ludlam, Ronald Tavel

ANIMATIONS: A TRILOGY FOR MABOU MINES/Lee Breuer

THE RED ROBINS/Kenneth Koch

THE WOMEN'S PROJECT/Penelope Gilliatt, Lavonne Mueller, Rose Leiman Goldemberg, Joyce Aaron-Luna Tarlo, Kathleen Collins, Joan Schenkar, Phyllis Purscell

WORDPLAYS: NEW AMERICAN DRAMA/Maria Irene Fornes, Ronald Tavel, Jean-Claude van Itallie, Richard Nelson, William Hauptman, John Wellman

BEELZEBUB SONATA/Stanislaw I. Witkiewicz

DIVISION STREET AND OTHER PLAYS/Steve Tesich

TABLE SETTINGS/James Lapine

THE PRESIDENT AND EVE OF RETIREMENT/Thomas Bernhard

TWELVE DREAMS

LIBRARY OF CONGRESS CATALOGING IN PUBLICATION DATA
Twelve Dreams
Library of Congress Catalog Card No.: 82-81974
ISBN: 0-933826-33-8

Printed in the United States of America

TWELVE DREAMS

a play by

James Lapine

Performing Arts Journal Publications
New York

For Phyllis, Mark and Larry

Publication of this book has been made possible in part by grants received from the National Endowment for the Arts, Washington, D.C., a federal agency, and the New York State Council on the Arts.

Twelve Dreams opened at The Public Theatre/Martinson Hall in New York City on December 1, 1981, as a New York Shakespeare Festival production, Joseph Papp, producer. It was directed by the author, with scenery by Heidi Landesman, costumes by William Ivey Long, lighting by Frances Aronson, and music by Allen Shawn. The cast was as follows:

CHARLES HATRICK	*James Olson*
EMMA HATRICK	*Olivia Laurel Mates*
JENNY	*Marcell Rosenblatt*
PROFESSOR	*Stefan Schnabel*
SANFORD PUTNAM	*Thomas Hulce*
DOROTHY TROWBRIDGE	*Carole Shelley*
MISS BANTON	*Valerie Mahaffey*
RINDY	*Stacy Glick*

AUTHOR'S NOTE: *Twelve Dreams* was inspired by a case study of Carl Jung's, as outlined in the book *Man and His Symbols*. Little information can be found to illuminate this record of a ten-year-old girl who, according to Jung's theory of the "collective unconscious," predicted her own death through a series of twelve dreams. This play takes these dreams as a starting point and all characters and events are fictional.

—JAMES LAPINE

CHARACTERS:

CHARLES HATRICK, a psychiatrist
EMMA HATRICK, his ten-year-old daughter
JENNY, Hatrick's cousin by marriage
PROFESSOR, a prominent European pyschiatrist
SANFORD PUTNAM, a student of pyschiatry
DOROTHY TROWBRIDGE, a patient of Dr. Hatrick
MISS BANTON, Emma's dance instructor
RINDY, Emma's best friend

The setting is a university town in New England.

The action of the play takes place in the Hatrick house which consists of a front-porch and entryway, a parlor area, the Doctor's office/study, a staircase to a second level where there is a long hallway that leads to Emma's bedroom. There is also an exterior area to the house where in the second act a swing hangs.

ACT I: Winter, 1936
ACT II: Spring, 1937

EMMA'S TWELVE DREAMS

[I]   Once upon a time there was a bunch of small animals. They came together and frightened me. They grew to a tremendous size and swallowed me up.

[II]   Once upon a time there was a very drunk woman who fell into a lake. But when she came out all wet, she wasn't drunk at all.

[III]   Once upon a time there was a bad boy who threw mud at all the people walking by, and then all of the people became bad.

[IV]   Once upon a time there was a big evil animal that looked like a snake monster. One day the monster appeared and swallowed all the little animals around, but then God came out of the four corners of the room and killed the monster and freed all the little animals from inside.

[V]   Once upon a time I went into heaven where all of these weird and disgusting dances were being performed. Then I fled to Red Hell and saw angels being nice.

[VI]   Once upon a time I saw a drop of water in my microscope and there were all kinds of tree branches in the water.

[VII]   Once upon a time my pet mouse was penetrated by worms, snakes, fishes, and people. Suddenly the mouse becomes human.

[VIII]   Once upon a time I was very ill. Suddenly all of these birds came out of my skin and began to cover me completely.

[IX]   Once upon a time I was on the moon where there was a desert. And I started to sink real deep into the sand and the next thing I knew I was in Hell, where everything was red and hot.

[X]   Once upon a time there was a group of people who went on a picnic in Europe. But they decided to rest on an ant heap and then they got attacked. I got very upset by this and had to run into the river.

[XI]   Once upon a time I saw this big round lighted ball. I touched it and vapors came out of it. All of a sudden, a man came and killed me.

[XII]   Once upon a time, swarms of gnats covered up the sun, the moon and all of the stars in the sky except one. That star fell from the sky and landed on a pretty little dreamer.

Each of the twelve dreams is either dramatized or referred to directly within the play. The dreams appear on the page numbers indicated above, and are marked in the text with the corresponding roman numerals.

ACT I

Scene 1

Music. Enter Hatrick in a smoking jacket. He carries Emma's dream book and walks to his study where he sits and examines it. Enter Jenny and Emma on the second level. Jenny escorts Emma to bed, then exits. Enter Professor. He comes downstage to an area separate from the house. He assumes the position of a lecturer. As the music and house lights fade, he begins to speak directly to the audience.

PROFESSOR: (*Squinting into the light.*) Could you please ask the question again—I am a slow listener. (*Pause.*) Yes. Of course I miss Christmas in my country and yes, it is true to a certain degree that I am not a religious person . . . at least religious in the sense that you use the word. However, I believe that religion is a great link to the past! What is interesting about Christmas—and what is so often forgotten, is that Christmas comes at the darkest time of the year. The Christmas tree, which you Americans have now managed to reproduce synthetically—the "evergreen"—is the only tree to remain green through this dark period.

(*Jenny enters the study carrying a silver tray, and tea pot. She notices Hatrick reading in the dark and turns on his reading light. She then pours him a cup of tea and exits.*)

PROFESSOR: The decoration of lights symbolizes the lighting up of darkness! I like to think that I make a profession of lighting up the darkness—in a manner of speaking of course. (*Pause. With amusement.*) Well, yes of course, men and women are different in America than in my country, or for that matter all of Europe and the rest of the world. It seems though here, if my perceptions are correct, that men and women are directing their greatest energies everywhere except toward their relationships with each other.

(*Jenny reappears on the second floor. She tiptoes into Emma's bedroom and tucks her in. She rearranges a few objects and exits.*)

PROFESSOR: Everyone is always running here, hardly leaving time to catch one's breath, which of course, allows for little introspection and intercourse. (*Pause.*) Why the titters? (*Pause.*) Oh. (*Annoyed.*) Intercourse as in the exchange of ideas. I'm not certain of the other.

(*Music. The back wall of Emma's bedroom is of a scrim material. Slowly lights rise behind it revealing a ballerina [Banton] on toe. She mechanically dances, as a ballerina in a music box might, twisting back and forth. The Professor pauses to gaze up at her, then turns to respond to the next question.*)

PROFESSOR: Indeed, I do think we give short shrift to our intuitive selves. Like the sedimentary layers of the earth we stand on, so does the human mind contain layers that date back far beyond our own experiences. None of us knows what we really know! (*Music fades, as do lights and the ballerina disappears.*) We must shut off our overly trained intellects and get in touch with our other parts. My experiences with the American Indians have been a great factor in my theoretical formulations.

(*Emma rises from her bed, grabs her bird book, and slowly walks from her room, down the stairs, directly to the Professor. She gets to him just as he completes his speech.*)

PROFESSOR: The Indian knows to think with the heart not the head. When the Pueblo Indian meets a stranger for instance, they ask . . . what animal is this? There was great difficulty in their deciding which animal to assign me. One day I had to climb a ladder to enter one of their structures. Well, I did so—but while the Indians climb up backwards, I climbed up the normal European fashion, facing the ladder. When I did this, a great shout came forth. A bear! A bear! (*He laughs.*) They thought I was a bear.

[I]

(*He turns and lets out a loud bear roar in Emma's direction. Startled, she backs off, but he continues growling and advances toward her. His noise is joined by the other characters, each of whom enters taking on the likeness and sounds of an animal: Jenny, a billy goat; Banton, a horse. Hatrick remains in his seat as the group converge around Emma. Their animal noises grow in volume and intensity, then suddenly break into a peal of laughter. Hatrick has grabbed a tray with a bottle and glasses and has come*) *behind the group. Trowbridge, Banton and Rindy make a speedy exit.*)

(*As the lights come up slowly, Hatrick pours Professor and Putnam drinks. Jenny takes the tray from him and goes to the side with Emma. There is simultaneous conversation that approximates the following . . .*)

H: Well, I've been saving this sherry for you.

P: This is very good sherry Charles.

PR: I am flattered Charles.

H: This visit of yours has been much too long in the coming.

P: This is a rare sight, Professor.

PR: Well, I hope I haven't intruded on your holidays in any way.

H: On the contrary, you're making it a more festive occasion.

J: It's getting awfully late young lady.

E: Oh Jenny, can't I sit and visit for a little while.

J: Emma, you've been up late every night this week.

E: But I'm not tired.

J: All right, but just for a little while longer. And no story either.

E: Okay, but I really wish I could have a story too.

J: Maybe tomorrow night!

PUTNAM: (*To Jenny.*) Excuse me. Another glass please. (*Professor and Hatrick sit.*)

PROFESSOR: Well, Charles, this house of yours is certainly decked in the Christmas spirit.

HATRICK: Emma and Jenny manage to escalate our celebration from year to year.

EMMA: (*Goes and sits on Hatrick's lap.*) Daddy doesn't believe in Christmas.

HATRICK: Not exactly, Emma . . .

PROFESSOR: Well, Christmas seems to be doing wonders for the economy.

HATRICK: Not mine. (*Professor laughs . . . perhaps too loudly. Jenny shakes her head and exits.*)

PUTNAM: How did you feel about today's lectures, Professor?

HATRICK: Sanford . . .

PROFESSOR: Why, Mr. Putnam, I thought they went very well.

PUTNAM: You mean you're not disturbed by the resistance to some of your new thinking? (*He pours himself another drink, then positions himself between the two.*)

PROFESSOR: Not at all, my boy, not at all. It is difficult for some to hear contrary opinions—I guess you might say that a new idea upsets them.

HATRICK: (*Apologetic.*) I just don't think it was quite what the committee had in mind when they invited you.

PUTNAM: Well, how do you respond when some of the doctors at the university suggest your ideas are not within the realm of science?

HATRICK: (*Annoyed.*) Sanford, this is a social visit. Let's not grill the doctor anymore.

PROFESSOR: Hogwash! My ideas and theories are documented from experience. I have never claimed that they came to me by divine revelation. Tell me again your position, Mr. Putnam.

PUTNAM: I am the youngest resident in psychiatry at the clinic and Charles is my adviser.

PROFESSOR: Ah hah . . .

PUTNAM: Charles and I were both very interested in your early theories.

HATRICK: And we're still interested in your theories.

PROFESSOR: Thank you. I've known Charles for many years. Since his training.

EMMA: How long ago was that, Professor?

PROFESSOR: Oh, Emma, that was a long, long time ago. Your Daddy was a fine student.

PUTNAM: And I'm Charles' best student.

PROFESSOR: Ah, and modest too, I can see, Mr. Putnam. (*Hatrick and Professor exchange a knowing chuckle.*)

PUTNAM: Professor, that business you got into today about the Indians —I thought Dr. Winston would just slide off his chair. You can't really believe that?

HATRICK: Sanford . . .

PUTNAM: Some of the faculty were saying that you were just spinning those tales to stir up some controversy.

HATRICK: (*Flying off the handle.*) MR. PUTNAM! What is it with you? I specifically asked that we not discuss the lectures! (Putnam recoils.)

PROFESSOR: (*Embarrassed.*) It's quite all right Charles, really . . .

HATRICK: (*Pulling back.*) Well, I for one am very glad to have you back for a visit. It's been much too long since we've had the occasion for a face to face exchange . . . and letter writing has become one—

PUTNAM: (*Indignant.*) You'll have to excuse me, Professor. I feel I have over stayed my welcome. (*Looks at Hatrick. Then grabs his coat and flies out the front door, slamming it behind him.*)

HATRICK: I am sorry.

PROFESSOR: (*Chuckling.*) Quite a high-strung young man.

EMMA: Daddy, Mr. Putnam had three glasses.

HATRICK: Did he? . . . well, he is very bright, but a little lacking in the manners department.

PROFESSOR: A case of arrested development . . . huh, Charles? (*They chuckle.*)

EMMA: I like Mr. Putnam, Daddy.

HATRICK: So do we Emma.

PROFESSOR: So, Emma, I bet you got a lot of nice gifts for Christmas?

EMMA: (*Shy.*) Yes.

PROFESSOR: What was your favorite?

EMMA: (*Shrugs.*) I guess this bird book and the recording that goes along with it.

HATRICK: Emma gave some pretty wonderful gifts, too.

PROFESSOR: Come over here, Emma. (*She does so.*) There's a little package in the hallway all wrapped up. There's a surprise inside for you.

(*Emma dashes to the hallway as Jenny enters.*)

JENNY: Professor, your things are in the guest room and I have prepared a light supper for you if you wish.

PROFESSOR: Well, I hope you haven't burned the pot roast like you did on my last visit. (*He laughs.*)

JENNY: (*Not amused.*) We're having cold cuts.

(*Emma enters, excited, carrying wrapping paper and a stuffed teddy bear.*)

EMMA: Jenny, look! A stuffed animal. Oh, thank you, Professor.

(*Emma gives him a kiss, then pulls Jenny over to show her and Hatrick the gift. Professor leans over and pats Jenny's ass. She is startled and stiffens.*)

PROFESSOR: (*Chuckles.*) Well, the cold cuts are getting cold, right Jenny? (*He heads off to dining room.*) And I'm famished. Emma, are you going to join us?

JENNY: (*Cold.*) Emma has already had her supper.

(*Professor continues talking and heads toward the dining room. Jenny lets Hatrick know her displeasure with a stare. Hatrick shrugs his shoulders and heads off after the houseguest.*)

[II]

(*Music. Lights. Enter Dorothy Trowbridge drunk, carrying her shoes and a Christmas gift, humming a children's tune and laughing uncontrollably. She staggers to the parlor area, where Emma sits and watches in amazement. Lighting or projections suggest water. Trowbridge loses her balance and collapses. Emma goes to her, "Wake up . . . get up . . . are you okay?" Trowbridge pops up and frightens Emma with a "Boo!" She then lets out a laugh that turns to a moan of pain and collapses again as the Pro-*

fessor enters carrying an empty bucket. He begins speaking in German as he approaches Trowbridge. He examines her before throwing the bucket towards her as if it were filled with water. Lights change and Trowbridge reacts as if she has just been doused. Professor exits as she gets up. Embarrassed, she stares at the child for a moment, shakes herself off, puts her shoes on, and walks to the side entrance of the doctor's study with a steady foot. Emma exits.)

Scene 2

(Hatrick is in his study. Trowbridge collects herself outside the entry—hiding the gift she rushes into the study.)

TROWBRIDGE: I'm sorry I'm late doctor. Trouble with my driver. (*She sits.*)

HATRICK: Mrs. Trowbridge, I notice you're often late for your visits—

TROWBRIDGE: (*Curtly.*) Now don't you start up with me doctor. I always pay you for a full hour!

HATRICK: Yes, but the—(*Trowbridge pulls out a gift and holds it out to Hatrick.*)

TROWBRIDGE: Merry Christmas . . . (*Hatrick is suprised for a moment. Then annoyed, takes the gift.*)

HATRICK: Thank you. (*He takes it over to his desk where he puts it down.*)

TROWBRIDGE: If you don't like it you can . . . (*Annoyed that he doesn't open the gift, she begins to chatter at a great speed.*) I have had *such* an exasperating day. We were at the Kessler's—the Harry Kessler's, of the steel fortune. We stopped by to exchange gifts—we usually exchange gifts on Christmas Day, but they had been out of town until now. Well, I shopped and shopped for their gift and then Harry had the audacity to tell me our gift was not to their liking. I mean I was so angry I could hardly control myself. I immediately told them I had a splitting headache and George and I excused ourselves and left their house. (*As she lights a cigarette.*) Do you mind if I smoke? (*She motions for him to bring her an ashtray.*) Maybe he didn't intentionally offend me. He was very apologetic and we did have a great many egg nogs. (*Hatrick brings her the ashtray.*) Oh, thank you!

HATRICK: Did Mr. Kessler actually say that he didn't like the gift?

TROWBRIDGE: He said he thought perhaps a donation to charity was something to consider for future exchanges—now isn't that ridiculous! What kind of gift is that?

HATRICK: Well, Mrs. Trowbridge, I . . .

TROWBRIDGE: It has been such a difficult week. The holidays and all. (*She gets up and begins pacing the room.*) The stores being so crowded and what not—so many social engagements. I don't know how a person is supposed to put up with the pressure. Never knowing what to buy— how to please who.

HATRICK: Mrs. Trowbridge. (*Points to chair.*) Please. (*Annoyed, she goes back and sits.*) Now. What was Christmas like at your house as a child?

TROWBRIDGE: (*Angry.*) Christmas was a very happy time. (*Pause. Emma and Rindy enter the parlor with dolls in hand. They sit and play.*) Mamma would decorate the house with holly and mistletoe and the banisters would be lined with evergreen and the entire house would smell as if a forest had been brought inside.

HATRICK: What else?

TROWBRIDGE: Oh everything was *so* pretty at Christmas—the special foods and parties—one knew what to expect. (*Pause.*) I don't know. This has been a most miserable holiday—no excitement, no surprises. That Kessler gift was *the most* extraordinary candy dish — mother-of-pearl — it cost a small fortune. Damned if I'll buy them another gift! Why do these things always happen to me doctor? And now I'm not feeling very well . . . (*She gets up again and begins to pace.*)

(*Parlor.*)

EMMA: Sometimes I wish my doll had long hair like Miss Banton's.

RINDY: She's so pretty.

EMMA: I know.

RINDY: But she never opens her mouth except to yell out positions. She's so queer.

EMMA: She's just shy, Rindy.

RINDY: (*Pointing to Emma's doll.*) Where did you get that?

EMMA: Jenny gave it to me for my birthday.

RINDY: This is so boring. I hate dolls Emma. They're stupid! Let's get one of your father's books.

EMMA: Rindy, no!

RINDY: Why not? You like them as much as I do. I know you do. (*She pulls Emma up and drags her off stage.*)

EMMA: Rindy! (*They exit.*)

HATRICK: Please, can you be more specific about what made you happy at Christmas?

TROWBRIDGE: God, what an idiotic question! I was a child. Isn't one always happier as a child? Especially at Christmas? I am not happy now because of my health. And you doctors are of no help. We pay you a fortune and so rarely are we ever relieved of our pain.

HATRICK: You were only happy as a child?

TROWBRIDGE: (*Laughing.*) Oh, that is not fair. (*She rises.*) I am just not myself today. My driver is waiting.
HATRICK: Mrs. Trowbridge, don't get up—
TROWBRIDGE: Really, I cannot stay another moment—
HATRICK: You seem to feel you have to run away—
TROWBRIDGE: (*Exiting.*) I shall see you Tuesday and you shall tell me how I am.

(*Trowbridge makes a speedy exit before Hatrick can stop her; Emma and Rindy come into the parlor giggling as they look at the medical book. They sit and laugh hysterically; Jenny is seen entering the front door with a shopping bag. She overhears the girls before entering the parlor.*)

EMMA: Oooo, that's so disgusting.
RINDY: Look at that woman. She's got all those ugly bumps.
EMMA: She looks like you.
RINDY: She does not. Oh, oh oh, look at that man.
EMMA: It's disgusting. Quick, turn the page.
JENNY: Emma, where did you get that book?
EMMA: (*Panicked.*) Rindy got it out of Father's study.
RINDY: That's not true. You got it out and you know it.
EMMA: I did not! (*They begin to fight.*)
JENNY: Girls! No arguing. Give me that. (*Takes book. Looks at it in amazement and disgust.*) Why in heavens name do you want to look at these unfortunate people?
RINDY: Well, we just wanted to find out what's under our skin . . .
JENNY: What is under your skin?
RINDY: I want to go home.
JENNY: That can be arranged. (*Jenny takes Rindy's hand and they begin to exit.*)
EMMA: Jenny . . . please don't tell Father.
JENNY: (*Pause.*) We'll see about that. (*Jenny exits with Rindy.*)

[III]

(*Professor enters to Emma's side, repeating over and over . . .*)

PROFESSOR: Emma, I love that marvelous bird book you got for Christmas. And that bird record . . . oh, that bird record.

(*Enter Trowbridge to Emma repeating over and over . . .*)

TROWBRIDGE: Come give me a kiss, Emma. You are such a beautiful little girl. Come over here and give me a kiss.

(*Enter Putnam, to Emma, repeating over and over . . .*)

PUTNAM: You see, Emma, people tell me their dreams and I tell them what they mean. But, sometimes I can't tell.

(*Enter Jenny, repeating.*)

JENNY: It's time to wake up Emma. It's a lovely day outside. It's time to wake up and get dressed.

(*Enter Banton, repeating.*)

BANTON: Are you coming to class today Emma? Do you have your dance clothes, too?

(*Each of these lines is delivered with great affection to Emma. Rindy enters after Banton, her outfit now transformed to that of a boy's. She carries a bucket, dipping into it and smearing each of the cast. As they are touched they stop for a second and begin whispering Emma's name in an evil and seductive manner. Slowly, they close in on her, fighting among themselves to get Emma's attention. Blackout.*)

Scene 3

(*Hatrick and Professor in the parlor.*)

PROFESSOR: We live in a time of tribal leaders, we do. Hitler, Mussolini, Stalin and of course your Roosevelt. It is a disturbing time.

HATRICK: Why?

PROFESSOR: There is a desperation for leadership, I suppose. A need to relinquish individual responsibilities—people want to follow.

HATRICK: I'm embarrassed to admit I find myself very distant from the politics of the day—somehow events seem so far beyond an individual's control.

PROFESSOR: And they will become more so. Here everyone seems to be trying to keep up with his neighbor—a country made up of immigrants has created an atmosphere that forces the foreigner to give up his heritage. One cannot abandon a personality without paying a price.

HATRICK: There does seem to be a change in the nature of the patients in the clinic.

PROFESSOR: (*Excited.*) Oh, yes?

(*Emma enters wearing pajamas.*)

HATRICK: Well, look who's here. Ready for bed?

EMMA: (*Sits on her father's lap.*) No.

PROFESSOR: Do you mind if we continue our doctor talk?

EMMA: No, as long as I can listen.

PROFESSOR: (*Chuckling.*) What of the clinic, Charles?

HATRICK: There's an increasing number of people coming in and show-ing a dissatisfaction and unhappiness with life—nothing specific, no symptoms like we were trained to treat. Not the traditional hysteria.

PROFESSOR: Yes. I am not surprised. We are the products of our age and are in store for an entirely new range of mental disorders.

HATRICK: Well, that should be good for business.

PROFESSOR: (*Serious.*) One day we may have practices just like dentists.

HATRICK: Sometimes I wish I had a drill . . .

(*Jenny enters.*)

JENNY: Emma, I think it's time for you to go to bed.

EMMA: Do I have to?

HATRICK: Emma . . .

EMMA: All right. Good night, Papa. (*Kisses him.*) Good night, Doctor.

(*Jenny and Emma exit. Emma goes to her room where she plays with a telescope.*)

PROFESSOR: She's a wonderful little girl, Charles. Unusual.

HATRICK: That she is. I want you to look at something. You will appre-ciate this. For Christmas, other children buy their fathers a tie, slippers, a pipe. Emma, like a good psychiatrist's child makes me a book of her dreams—because I "like books most of all"—and damn if they're not the most peculiar assortment I've ever seen. Here look. (*Opens book and reads.*)

[IV]

"Once upon a time, there was a big evil animal that looked like a snake-monster. One day the monster appeared and swallowed all the little animals around, but then God came out of the four corners of the room and killed the monster and freed all the little animals from inside."

PROFESSOR: (*Amused.*) How very odd. Are these dreams Emma had after her mother's death?

HATRICK: No. The irony is that these past four years, Emma has made that adjustment far better than I.

PROFESSOR: Yes. Tell me Charles, to change the subject for a moment. Are you feeling well? Are you all right?

HATRICK: (*Taken off guard.*) That's not a question I've been asking my-self recently.

PROFESSOR: Well, if I may say so, you have seemed a bit preoccupied this visit.

HATRICK: I'm sorry. I don't mean to be.

PROFESSOR: (*Studying him momentarily.*) There is no reason to apolo-gize. Perhaps you have just caught the holiday blues from your patients. (*Takes book from Hatrick.*) May I look at this?

HATRICK: I wish you would. I can find no context for these images. Not a personal association.

PROFESSOR: Well, you know me. This is my favorite kind of reading.

HATRICK: And so short! (*They both laugh.*)

(*Emma's bedroom.*)

JENNY: Emma, let's get into bed.

EMMA: I'm trying to find Orion's belt.

JENNY: (*Emphatically.*) Emma . . .

EMMA: Do you think anyone lives in space?

JENNY: No. I don't.

EMMA: But isn't that where heaven is?

JENNY: No one is sure where heaven is.

EMMA: But if it's not in space, where is it? (*No answer.*) I don't think Daddy believes there is a heaven.

JENNY: Why not?

EMMA: When I told him you said that was where Mommy was, he said you didn't have that information.

JENNY: (*Annoyed.*) Emma! Bed.

EMMA: Okay. (*Gets into bed.*) Jenny, I have an itch on my back. Would you scratch it for me?

JENNY: You seem to always have an itch around this time.

EMMA: Please . . .

JENNY: Okay. (*Jenny rubs Emma's back.*)

EMMA: Jenny, did my mother dress like Miss Banton or Mrs. Trowbridge?

JENNY: (*Alarmed.*) How do you know Mrs. Trowbridge's name?

EMMA: (*Flippant.*) I just heard it one day.

JENNY: (*Grabbing her in anger.*) You have very big ears, young lady, and if you're not careful, somebody's going to snip them off!

EMMA: I'm sorry.

JENNY: (*Cools down and continues to rub Emma's back.*) No. Your mother did not dress like either of them. She was a very stylish woman though, Emma. Sometimes when we were growing up, I would get some of her "hand-me-downs." (*Joking.*) Unfortunately, they never looked quite the same on me.

EMMA: Am I going to look like her?

JENNY: Well, you have your mother's eyes, and I think our family's smile, but in many ways, you are your father's little girl.

EMMA: And what did Mother die from?

JENNY: (*Hesitant.*) She was very sick and she just died.

EMMA: Well, why do some people die and other's don't?

JENNY: Emma, everyone dies. Some just die sooner than others.

EMMA: Did God make her die?

JENNY: (*Rubbing Emma's back.*) Emma, I think you should have this discussion with your father. Now stop with your endless questions.

EMMA: I'm sorry.

JENNY: (*Tucking her in.*) One thing is for sure. You have your father's mind.

EMMA: What kind of mind do you have, Jenny?

JENNY: At the moment, a very tired one. Now enough of this conversation. Say your prayers and I'll tuck you in. (*Music.*)

EMMA: Spread out they wings, Lord Jesus mild,
And take to thee thy chick, thy child,
If Satan would devour it,
No harm shall overpower it,
So let the angels sing!

JENNY: Sleep tight, Emma. Sweet dreams. (*She kisses her.*)

EMMA: Good night, Jenny.

JENNY: Don't let the bed bugs bite!

(*Emma giggles, as lights go to black.*)

Scene 4

(*Banton and Rindy are dressed in dance attire; they are doing warm-up exercises as they speak.*)

BANTON: Okay, Rindy, we'll do the same exercises we did last week. Now watch yourself in the mirror . . . and one, two, three, four . . . and one, two, three, four . . .

RINDY: Miss Banton, why aren't you married?

BANTON: (*Flustered.*) What a question to ask.

RINDY: I'm curious.

BANTON: I know you're curious. You shouldn't intrude on the privacy of others! (*Pause.*) I was married, but I'm not married anymore.

RINDY: (*Excited.*) You were? What happened?

BANTON: It didn't work out.

RINDY: Were you unhappy?

BANTON: Yes and it doesn't make me very happy right now to talk about it either . . .

RINDY: I'm sorry. It's just that you're so pretty—Emma and I think you're the prettiest woman we've ever seen.

BANTON: (*Embarrassed.*) Thank you. Next exercise. (*She helps her begin a new movement.*)

RINDY: Emma's father is looking for a wife. Maybe you would like him.

BANTON: (*Laughing.*) Life is a little more complicated than that young lady.

RINDY: I don't think life is complicated.

BANTON: That's one of the pleasures of being your age. One day your life will be complicated too.

RINDY: I'm going to be a prima ballerina when I grow up, and I'll dance before all kinds of fancy people and they'll bring me flowers backstage with notes from handsome men.

BANTON: (*Cracking up.*) You're really a character.

RINDY: I'm not trying to be.

BANTON: You just stay the way you are. Now let's begin. We can't wait for Emma. (*Taking her to dance area.*) Are you going to be a wonderful little swan?

RINDY: Uh huh.

[V]

(*Music. Banton and Rindy begin a lovely balletic dance. Emma joins them and is gently scolded for being late. The dance suggests a feeling of innocence and fun, and the three chatter and giggle throughout. The music begins to change in tone as Banton places the girls in angelic poses. As she continues to touch the girls, there begins a subtle change in her attitude. The touching becomes almost seductive and sexual and the girls begin to stiffen under her hand and exchange nervous glances. Banton then slowly leaves the girls, returning to her ballerina position behind the scrim where she begins to take off her clothes. The girls break from their pose and watch in disbelief.*)

(*The sweet music of the exercises has now become a rather sinister melody, as Banton goes into a lewd and frenetic dance. She tears from the second level down the stairs. In a fury, the girls pick up her clothes and disappear on the second level as Banton runs rampant through the study, and then to the parlor. Banton, exhausted, collapses in the parlor as the girls reappear through a trap door that is under the rug in the study. They slowly approach Banton carrying her clothes and they attempt to dress her, as they might one of Emma's dolls. In the background Trowbridge and Hatrick enter and take their usual positions in the study. The girls get Banton up and slowly help her off-stage as*) *the music fades and the lights come up on the study.*)

Scene 5

TROWBRIDGE: . . . I remember the smell of cigars. It bothered me for some time, but then I came to love the smell. George smokes cigars. Anyway, Father would sometimes get in very heated arguments with this one or that one, but he would never raise his voice. Sometimes I would fall asleep right there in his lap, and he or Mama would carry me to bed. No, Papa seldom got angry.

HATRICK: And how about you, Mrs. Trowbridge?

TROWBRIDGE: I am like him in that respect.

HATRICK: You never get angry? Haven't you been angry with me?

TROWBRIDGE: (*Curt.*) I never raise my voice. I never shout! (*Pause.*) Father and Mother were very civilized. Well-mannered. They would be most confused to know I was seeing a psychiatrist. No, they were always in good spirits.

HATRICK: Always in good spirits? They never had arguments or disagreements?

TROWBRIDGE: There were moments when Mama and Papa disagreed, but Mamma always deferred to Papa. He ran a tight ship—no George would never be as stern to me as Papa was to Mama.

HATRICK: What of their disagreements. What did they concern?

TROWBRIDGE: Family matters mostly.

HATRICK: Yes? Be more specific.

TROWBRIDGE: Oh, you know. Once I was playing in the parlor—running about, and I knocked over a lovely Limoges lamp of Mama's. She was furious . . .

HATRICK: Yes. What else?

TROWBRIDGE: Let's see. I remember that I snuck into Papa's desk once —Lord knows why—and mucked about with his things. He was fit to be tied! Hmmm . . . on occasion, they did not approve of some of my friends. Like the time when I had a crush on a very handsome young man. Papa certainly did not approve of that. (*Nervous giggle.*) And let's see, what else—

HATRICK: Why didn't he approve?

TROWBRIDGE: The young man was not of our social class.

HATRICK: How did you meet him?

TROWBRIDGE: He worked for Father.

HATRICK: And what happened?

TROWBRIDGE: (*Sharp.*) It ended.

HATRICK: How did you feel about that?

TROWBRIDGE: (*Angry, she gets out of chair.*) Does this have anything to do with my unhappiness, Doctor? Isn't that what you're to deal with?

HATRICK: (*Losing patience.*) Certainly, Mrs. Trowbridge. What is it about your unhappiness?

TROWBRIDGE: (*Yelling at him.*) WELL, IF I COULD UNDERSTAND MY UNHAPPINESS I CERTAINLY WOULDN'T BE HERE NOW! (*She is shocked by her own anger and pulls away.*)

HATRICK: (*Trying to soothe her.*) There is a connection between your past and present feelings. In our first visit you discussed your inability to see things through—your one and only visit to each of the other psychiatrists—your impatience in various social situations. Let's try and find out where this impatience has its root.

TROWBRIDGE: (*Disconnected.*) I see your child when I come here. I marvel at that child . . . she sits in your parlor for hours, always absorbed in something. How old is she?

HATRICK: Why do you ask?

TROWBRIDGE: Why do you always answer a question with another question? I asked because here I am a woman of . . . well, many years more than your daughter, and I can't sit still to read the evening's paper. Just the other night we went to the opening of the ballet. I insisted George get us tickets. I also insisted that we not sit in the loge . . . Well, after much finagling, he got us box seats. *Box seats!* George was quite pleased with himself, even though he can't stand the ballet. Well, I shopped for days . . . found *the most extraordinary* scarlet gown, and off we went. Well, the curtain had not been up for more than fifteen minutes when I had one of my attacks. An attack so severe mind you, that we had to leave before intermission . . . before we could exchange pleasantries with the most prominent citizens in town!

(*Jenny is on her way up the steps when she hears Mrs. Trowbridge and eavesdrops for a moment.*)

HATRICK: Describe these attacks again, please.

TROWBRIDGE: I TOLD YOU I CAN'T. They are so unpleasant that one can hardly explain them. They're like a nightmare. The most horrible and painful feeling one has ever experienced. No doctor has been able to diagnose them—well, you know all about that.

HATRICK: Tell me where you feel the pain.

TROWBRIDGE: My head, my back aches so . . . and pain in the pelvic region. I could barely stand up straight. I sobbed the entire way home. Everyone saw us leave!

(*Jenny exits up steps.*)

HATRICK: How often have you had these attacks?
TROWBRIDGE: Often. What time do you have Doctor?
HATRICK: We have a few minutes left.
TROWBRIDGE: (*Rising.*) No. I really must run.
HATRICK: (*Calling to her as she begins to exit.*) Mrs. Trowbridge . . .
TROWBRIDGE: (*On exit.*) No!

(*Trowbridge exits. Hatrick sits for a moment exasperated, then exits.*)

[VI]

(*Music. Emma enters the parlor and sits staring at her watch. Rindy enters the landing area. She is wearing a fur stole, lipstick, high heels, pocketbook, etc. She dolls herself up like Trowbridge, then enters and sits.*)

RINDY: Oh my God, I'm so late. I'm so late.
EMMA: (*Scolding.*) You are always late. Now you just sit down.
RINDY: Well, of course I'm late. I'm nuts. What did you expect?
EMMA: You have to stop being nuts and be healthy. This is dumb!
RINDY: I can't be healthy because my head hurts.
EMMA: So why does it hurt?
RINDY: It hurts because we were at the ballet and I got a headache.
EMMA: What kind of a headache?
RINDY: A migrant headache.
EMMA: What did it feel like?
RINDY: It felt like my head was full of water.
EMMA: Your head was full of water?
RINDY: Uh huh. And a drop of water dripped out.
EMMA: A drop of water?
RINDY: A drop of water.
EMMA: A drop of water?
RINDY: A drop of water. (*Lights and music change.*) Suddenly there are tree
    branches in the water.
RINDY *and* EMMA: Elm trees, pine trees, spruce trees, poplar trees, oak
    trees, evergreen trees—all kinds.

(*Trowbridge and Banton enter from opposite sides, and stand at the edge of the parlor; Jenny enters from the rear and stands in the back of the parlor; Emma and Rindy alternate the names of the trees pointing them out to Trowbridge and Banton respectively; Trowbridge says "a drop" and holds her hand out to Emma—Banton says "of water" doing the same with Rindy; Jenny says "a drop of water" stretching her hands out to the girls, but they are pulled away from her by Trowbridge and Banton who embrace the girls leaving Jenny with arms extended alone in the center of the parlor as the lights fade to black.*)

Scene 6

(Emma playing on the floor with her doll's house in the parlor. Putnam enters as if coming from the outside.)

PUTNAM: Hello, Emma.

EMMA: *(Startled.)* Father's upstairs, but I think he will be down in a minute.

PUTNAM: I know. I saw you playing so I thought I would say hello. *(He sits and begins to read a book.)*

EMMA: Do you like wearing glasses?

PUTNAM: That's a very strange question. Hmm, I don't think I've ever given that much thought. I suppose if I had the choice I would choose to have perfect eyesight and never have to wear them.

EMMA: Sometimes I wish I wore them.

PUTNAM: Why?

EMMA: Do you have a wife?

PUTNAM. No, and what does that have to do with wearing glasses?

EMMA: I guess I really don't want to wear glasses because they would be hard to dance with.

PUTNAM: Emma, do you have a boyfriend?

EMMA: *(Giggling.)* No, of course not. I'm too young. Someday I will. Do you want to see my doll's house?

PUTNAM: Certainly.

EMMA: I have a game. You close your eyes. I will put something in your hands and you tell me what it is.

PUTNAM: Okay!

(Putnam closes his eyes and Emma takes him by the hand sitting him down next to her. She takes a piece from the house and puts it in his hand.)

PUTNAM: Let's see. *(Examines it.)* I would say this feels like a bed.

EMMA: Right. I got it from Jenny for my birthday. Close your eyes again. *(Places another object in his hand.)*

PUTNAM: Hmm, this is certainly not a bed. Arms, legs, hair—I would almost be certain that this is a person—probably female, or a Scottish male. Can I open my eyes now?

EMMA: Yes, it's a little girl.

PUTNAM: What's her name?

(Jenny enters from the back, and pauses to overhear their conversation.)

EMMA: She doesn't have one.

PUTNAM: She doesn't have a name? That's not very fair!

EMMA: The world's not always fair.

PUTNAM: Who told you that?

EMMA: Jenny.

PUTNAM: And do you always believe everything Jenny says?

EMMA: Well, . . .

JENNY: (*Entering.*) Hello, Mr. Putnam . . . Emma, there's a surprise for you in the kitchen!

EMMA: (*Exiting.*) I know what it is!

JENNY: Yes, then upstairs for a bath. (*Annoyed.*) I would appreciate your knocking before entering this house. You gave me quite a start.

PUTNAM: Oh, I did knock. Then I walked in.

JENNY: Dr. Hatrick will be down in a moment. Would you care to wait in the study?

(*Putnam is absorbed in playing with the toys. Jenny moves downstage to him in amazement.*)

Excuse me.

(*She takes the toys away from him, except Putnam is able to hold on to one object.*)

You know, Mr. Putnam, I think Emma has a little crush on you.

PUTNAM: Me?

JENNY: You are the only other person in the room.

PUTNAM: Right . . .

JENNY: Have you any children?

PUTNAM: No. I'm not married.

JENNY: (*Has been watching him fiddle with Emma's toys.*) But you enjoy playing with doll's things.

PUTNAM: (*Loud, nervous laugh.*) Well, I wasn't—

(*Jenny goes to take the object away from Putnam, but he holds on to it, and the two are suddenly engaged in a tug-of-war. Hatrick enters from behind astounded by what he sees.*)

HATRICK: Good Lord!

(*The two let go. Embarrassed, Jenny takes the toys and exits.*)

HATRICK: Sanford, let's speak in the study.

(*Hatrick and Putnam go to the study.*)

HATRICK: (*Sarcastic.*) Thank you for coming over. (*They sit.*) I was very disturbed to hear about an unfortunate incident at the clinic, and I wanted to discuss it with you before too much time had passed.

PUTNAM: Oh no. You haven't been calling me because of that nonsense.

HATRICK: What happened?

PUTNAM: (*Put out.*) It's very simple. There's a manic-depressive woman on the ward. Her mother died recently and she went on a complete binge—running around to every bar in town, changing her outfit hour by hour—the usual. I was on the rounds with the eminent Dr. Winston. I was asking her a battery of questions and she insisted on answering each of my questions with a wise crack.

HATRICK: And?

PUTNAM: I said, "You seem rather happy for someone who has just lost their mother?"

HATRICK: And?

PUTNAM: The woman reacted hostilely and had to be restrained by an attendant. Winston exploded because I made the remark.

HATRICK: Well, don't you think he was justified?

PUTNAM: No. (*Hatrick shoots him a look.*) Okay, yes and no. Look, Charles, I enjoy the work, but frankly the patients are making far more sense than our colleagues. Do you realize someone actually saw Winston crawling around on his office floor this week.

HATRICK: Crawling?

PUTNAM: Yes, crawling! And I'm supposed to pay heed to his professorial attitude?

HATRICK: We're not talking about Dr. Winston, we're talking about you Mr. Putnam and you were wrong.

PUTNAM: I was not.

HATRICK: Your reputation for intelligence and knowledge is uncontested. However, your dealing so flippantly with an unstable person is a very serious issue.

PUTNAM: I asked her a question, Charles—

HATRICK: And what you can't seem to get through that head of yours is that although the question may make perfect sense, the manner in which you offer it is of equal importance.

PUTNAM: Please, . . .

HATRICK: You cannot drive a nail into a patient's most sensitive nerve in the course of your diagnostic quests!

PUTNAM: Charles, we've been over this—

HATRICK: People have to help themselves. You are being trained in psychiatry not surgery. You still have a great deal to learn about human nature, and you might begin by improving this cocky attitude of yours.

PUTNAM: My attitude will be much improved when the therapists who are crawling around their offices leave me alone with the patients. (*Putnam goes to sit down.*)

HATRICK: (*Curt.*) I have another appointment. Good day!
PUTNAM: (*Boiling.*) Good day.

(*Putnam storms out of the study, through the hallway and out the door where Banton is standing with a handful of clothes, about to knock. They both go flying to the floor, the clothes scattered about them.*)

PUTNAM: (*As he gets up.*) Oh, my god, I'm sorry. Are you all right?
BANTON: I think so. (*He awkwardly tries to help her up, doing more harm than good.*)
PUTNAM: I touched your breast!
BANTON: What?
PUTNAM: When I helped you up . . . I apologize.
BANTON: (*Angry.*) Are you Dr. Hatrick?
PUTNAM: Me? Dr. Hatrick? Please. At the moment I'd rather be Doctor Winston.
BANTON: Who's Dr. Winston?
PUTNAM: He's the one given to crawling fits.
BANTON: Huh?
PUTNAM: Who are you?
BANTON: I'm Eleanor Banton. Emma's dance instructor. Emma left some things at school and I happened to be in the neighborhood . . .
PUTNAM: Sweet kid, Emma. Peculiar, but cute.
BANTON: She's cute. (*Door opens and Jenny appears.*)
JENNY: Miss Banton . . .
BANTON: Hello. I was in the neighborhood . . . (*Hands her Emma's clothes; Putnam still hangs in the background.*)
JENNY: Thank you . . . Can I help you Mr. Putnam?
PUTNAM: Oh, no, thank you. Good night, ladies. (*Exits towards stage right. They watch him walk off.*)
JENNY: Was he annoying you?
BANTON: Oh no. We just had a little collision.
JENNY: I'm not surprised . . . that boy has a few loose screws if you ask me. (*Change of tone.*) Well, it was very thoughtful of you to drop these off. I would ask you in Miss Banton, but Emma's having a bath . . . and the Professor's here . . .
BANTON: Oh, no. Thank you very much. Really I must be getting home. (*She begins to exit.*)
JENNY: It's rather late for an unescorted young lady.
BANTON: It's really not that late.
JENNY: Oh . . . Well . . . thank you again for these . . . good night then.
BANTON: Goodnight.

(*Crosses stage right onto swing platform, Putnam leaps in front of her blocking her way. Startled she crosses her arms in front of her breasts for protection.*)

PUTNAM: Miss Banton, are you sure you're all right?

BANTON: If I discover any permanent injury, I'll see to it that you're the first to know.

PUTNAM: Thank you. Are you shy?

BANTON: I prefer to think of myself as quiet.

PUTNAM: I tend to be noisy.

BANTON: Obviously. Who are you?

PUTNAM: Oh God. Dr. Sanford Putnam. (*He puts his hand out to shake.*) Top of my class in medical school. The youngest resident in psychiatry in the history of the clinic.

BANTON: You're not shy.

PUTNAM: Actually I am. That accounts for my never shutting up when I'm nervous. I didn't speak until I was three. Everyone was concerned. Then at three I began speaking in complete sentences. I was reading by four. No one could believe it. By six I had read "The Iliad" and by the age of ten I was writing book reports on Boethius' philosophy. Being a dancer sounds exotic. Well, I don't really mean exotic, I mean interesting. Do you find it interesting? Well, obviously you do or you wouldn't do it. See, I don't like to dance—actually I never really have danced . . .

BANTON: You never really have danced?

PUTNAM: Maybe once at a wedding.

BANTON: Why that's just unbelievable.

PUTNAM: I like to read, you see . . .

BANTON: Dancing is very simple Mr. Putnam.

PUTNAM: Simple?

BANTON: Give me your hand.

PUTNAM: Give me your hand—give, give my hand to you?

BANTON: Yes.

(*She takes his hand and positions him for a social dance. She then takes her gloves off, then his glove and puts them in the pocket of his overcoat. Putnam gets more nervous by the moment. Just as she is about to get into position to dance, he breaks away.*)

PUTNAM: Wait. There's no music. This is not logical behavior.

BANTON: Dancing is a very logical activity.

PUTNAM: (*Mutters as she pulls him into dance position.*) Not for me . . .

(*She begins to instruct him in the art of dancing, at first with some resistance on his part. She counts a waltz "One, two, three . . ." We hear Hatrick and Professor talking and walking towards the study as Putnam and Banton freeze. She whispers in his ear, and then they exit.*)

Scene 7

(*Lights up as Hatrick and Professor walk into study. Hatrick pours drinks.*)

HATRICK: Sometimes I think that Putnam kid is inciting more mental illness than he's curing.

PROFESSOR: (*Chuckling.*) Charles, I'm afraid that Putnam kid is nothing more than young, ambitious and headstrong. Qualities that once might have been used to describe you.

HATRICK: I was never like that!

PROFESSOR: Well . . .

HATRICK: I can't believe I was ever like that.

PROFESSOR: A little bit of selective recall, Charles?

HATRICK: You never had to defend me. He has almost been expelled from the department two or three times. I'm beginning to wonder why I even put up with his nonsense.

PROFESSOR: Well, maybe he'll change course one day and become a pathologist.

HATRICK: Maybe. But he's very bright, and that would be a loss.

PROFESSOR: I'm told that there is a dearth of good pathologists.

HATRICK: And do you think good psychiatrists are easy to find? He told me Dr. Winston was discovered crawling around his office the other day.

PROFESSOR: (*Laughing.*) Is he still doing that?

HATRICK: You mean it's true?

PROFESSOR: Only when he's writing a paper. (*Serious.*) Have you seen his article on birth trauma? Fascinating theory.

HATRICK: Maybe we psychiatrists are all crazy. Emma told me the other day that Sanford reminded her of a chimp.

PROFESSOR: That's a perceptive observation. (*Pause.*)

HATRICK: So. I see you've brought back Emma's dream book. Did you have an opportunity to take a look at it?

PROFESSOR: Yes. I thought you might be asking me about them. Actually, I was very curious to know how they struck you.

HATRICK: Well, they have puzzled me.

PROFESSOR: I'm sure . . .

HATRICK: My first reaction was that these were simply the dreams of a child approaching puberty. Their ritualistic nature points to that. She's always been fascinated with animals and nature, so the images of the animals . . .

PROFESSOR: (*Grilling.*) These dreams are not about animals! These dreams are about destruction.

HATRICK: You mean, like the one about her being "dangerously ill. Suddenly birds come out of her skin and cover her completely . . .''

PROFESSOR: (*Serious.*) You've memorized them, haven't you?

HATRICK: Yes. (*Pause.*) Frankly, I didn't think all that much about them at first. Then it dawned on me how curious it was for Emma to give me such a gift. Again and again I unconsciously found myself going back to them. Studying them for some pattern or meaning.

PROFESSOR: And?

HATRICK: And, I have come to no conclusion. Please . . . what are your thoughts?

PROFESSOR: (*Enthusiastic.*) To be perfectly honest, I'm quite fascinated by these dreams. I too found myself drawn to them over again. The notions of death and rebirth, are puzzling.

[VII]

The animals being swallowed up and then reborn; the drop of water, the mouse that is penetrated by snakes and people, and then becomes human . . . they suggest some kind of genesis.

HATRICK: So you think the dreams are tied to Marjorie's death?

PROFESSOR: Perhaps. The death of a parent is an event that lodges in the psyche forever. But why are these images being cast up now? No, her preoccupation, as I see it, revolves around destruction and restoration—fundamental themes of worldly and human creation.

HATRICK: What is your point?

PROFESSOR: There is a symbolism here, complex and sophisticated, far beyond a child's knowledge—conscious knowledge, that is.

HATRICK: And?

PROFESSOR: And I ask myself, are these in fact dreams, or has someone been reading her books, or ancient mythology, or sending her to religious school—

HATRICK: (*Aggravated.*) Let's just consider that these are dreams. What do they suggest?

PROFESSOR: Well, to my thinking, these dreams seem to foretell the demise of the dreamer.

(*Hatrick drops his glass. There is a moment of silence. Switches to a more personal tone.*)

Look, Charles. This is all mere conjecture. I know you don't always agree with my theories! (*Desperate.*) God knows, if you want a Freudian explanation, we can certainly find an argument for some sexual manifestation. (*Laughs at his own inference.*) Seriously though, I would love to talk to Emma about these dreams before I leave tomorrow.

HATRICK: No! (*Takes dream book away from Professor.*) I'm going to have a little chat with her myself.

PROFESSOR: Can I at least sit in on this little chat.

HATRICK: No.

PROFESSOR: Well, no need to upset yourself. Dreams come to us for some reason. No doubt there will be an explanation. (*He stares at Hatrick for a moment. Then exits.*)

Scene 8

[VIII]

(*Emma has been in the parlor with her bird book. We hear the sound of bird calls in the background. Professor has gone into the hallway and returns carrying a doctor's bag and white gloves. He puts on the gloves as he converses with Emma.*)

PROFESSOR: Hello, Emma.

EMMA: Hello.

PROFESSOR: What are you doing?

EMMA: I'm listening to my birds and waiting for my friend Rindy to come visit.

PROFESSOR: Sounds like the white breasted nut hatch.

EMMA: No. It's the indigo bunting, but you were close.

PROFESSOR: Which is your favorite bird, Emma?

EMMA: I like finches, starling and tanangers. And I especially like owls . . . the kind that live at the top of towers.

PROFESSOR: Owls? (*He touches her and continues to do so in a menacing fashion.*) How have you been, Emma? I haven't seen you in ages. Did you have a good Christmas?

EMMA: Uh huh.

PROFESSOR: What kinds of gifts did you get?

EMMA: I got this bird book, and a microscope and slides to go with it. What's in that bag? (*Music.*)

PROFESSOR: Doctor's things.

EMMA: Do the things in that bag make people feel better?

PROFESSOR: Sometimes.

EMMA: I haven't been feeling very well lately.

PROFESSOR: Oh no? What seems to be the problem?

EMMA: Sometimes my chest hurts and I get headaches.

PROFESSOR: Well, well, well . . . let the Doctor take a look at you. (*He takes her hand; she tries to pull away.*)

EMMA: But I'm waiting for Rindy.
PROFESSOR: No! You're with me. (*He pulls her up.*) We'll just be a minute.

(*Professor takes Emma and slowly leads her up the staircase towards her bedroom. The bird sounds grow more menacing combining with music that suggests a waltz.*)

(*Hatrick continues looking at the book; lights come up behind the scrim revealing Putnam and Banton dancing; Jenny enters the parlor area and begins picking up after Emma; Rindy approaches the front door and knocks; Trowbridge approaches the study entrance, but then decides to go beyond it, and peeks into the parlor area where her eyes meet Jenny's in a moment of mutual panic.*)

(*Professor has got Emma into bed and begins examining her. She begins to complain of his touching when he begins to pull live birds from the bed. Emma screams as the birds appear.*)

(*Hearing the screams, each of the other characters turn and stare towards Emma's bedroom as music ends and lights black out on the appearance of the last bird.*)

ACT II

Scene 1

(*Music. Trowbridge and Hatrick enter study and chat. Emma plays on the swing with her doll. As the music ends, Trowbridge exits from the study and pulls herself together at the foot of the stairs. Emma notices her.*)

EMMA: Hello.

TROWBRIDGE: (*Startled and shy.*) Hello. (*They stare at each other for a moment.*)

EMMA: How did you get to be so rich?

TROWBRIDGE: (*Pause, then laughter.*) Just lucky, I guess. (*She moves closer.*) Do you wish you were very, very, very rich?

EMMA: I don't know . . .

TROWBRIDGE: What is your name?

EMMA: Emma.

TROWBRIDGE: Hello, Emma. May I sit down?

EMMA: Uh huh. What's your name?

TROWBRIDGE: Dorothy, but my friends call me Dottie. (*Trowbridge giggles. Emma looks about as if she were doing something wrong.*) What's the matter?

EMMA: Jenny will be very cross if she sees me sitting and talking to you.

TROWBRIDGE: Who's Jenny?

EMMA: She's almost my mother.

TROWBRIDGE: Almost?

EMMA: Uh huh. My mother's dead and Jenny's her cousin. She lives with us now.

TROWBRIDGE: And why should she be cross?

EMMA: She doesn't want me to see father's patients. I'm really supposed to be inside but it was so pretty out . . .

TROWBRIDGE: Yes, it is pretty . . . Well, I certainly don't want to get you in any trouble. (*She starts to get up, but Emma stops her.*)

EMMA: No. It's okay.

TROWBRIDGE: Guess what? I have a surprise. Do you like Hershey Kisses?

EMMA: I love them!

TROWBRIDGE: (*She pulls candy from her purse.*) Here's one for now, and one for later. (*The two gobble up the candy, giggling away.*)

EMMA: If you're so rich, why are you unhappy?

TROWBRIDGE: Who say's I'm unhappy?

EMMA: People who see my father are unhappy—and then he talks to them a lot and makes them feel better.

TROWBRIDGE: That simple, huh?

EMMA: You have such pretty clothes. You always wear something beautiful when you come to visit.

TROWBRIDGE: Why thank you.

EMMA: I love that scarf—it's so pretty.

TROWBRIDGE: This old thing? Had it for years—imported silk, very hard to come by these days! (*Trowbridge takes the scarf off and places it around Emma's neck.*)

EMMA: It's so soft.

TROWBRIDGE: (*Touching her face.*) Would you like to have it?

EMMA: (*Taking it off.*) Oh no, I couldn't take it.

TROWBRIDGE: Why not?

EMMA: Jenny would be very upset.

TROWBRIDGE: It would make me very happy if you kept it . . .

EMMA: I don't know Dottie . . .

(*We hear Jenny calling Emma from inside the house. Trowbridge darts up. Emma tries to return the scarf, but Trowbridge won't take it. As she exits, Emma quickly grabs the scarf and hides it just as Jenny comes out of the house towards her.*)

JENNY: Emma, you were supposed to play inside.

EMMA: I'm sorry. It was so pretty out today.

JENNY: Emma, were you just talking to someone out here?

EMMA: Only the birds, Jenny.

JENNY: I don't see any birds, Emma!

EMMA: I made them up!

JENNY: You made them up? (*Shakes her head.*) How would you like to talk to the green beans in the kitchen? They would very much like to have their ends snapped.

EMMA: (*Nervous until Jenny finally cracks a smile.*) You're so silly, Jenny.

JENNY: I'm silly . . .

(*Emma gets off the swing and dashes towards the house. Jenny is about to follow, but takes one last glance in the direction of Trowbridge's exit. As Emma walks to the front door, Jenny calls after her:*)

JENNY: Make sure you wash those hands!

(*Emma drops the scarf on her way into the house. As Jenny follows, she sees it, picks it up and hangs it in the hallway. At some point at the beginning of the scene, Hatrick has wandered into the parlor where he reads a book. Now Jenny joins Hatrick. She carries the evening paper.*)

JENNY: (*Sitting down.*) Charles. I'm sorry to bother you—I know how much you have on your mind these days . . .

HATRICK: What can I do for you?

JENNY: (*Nervous.*) There's something I would like to discuss with you.

HATRICK: Certainly.

JENNY: Charles . . . why do you allow these . . . crazy people to come into the house?

HATRICK: (*Amazed.*) What?

JENNY: These crazy people coming and going here—I don't think it's good for Emma, and I don't think Marjorie would have approved either.

HATRICK: (*Dismissing her.*) Jenny, there are no crazy people coming and going here.

JENNY: That Trowbridge woman flies in here two feet off the ground—

HATRICK: She comes in the study entrance—

JENNY: She circles around the house. She spies!

HATRICK: Jenny!

JENNY: (*Ominous.*) I saw her peeking through the window shade the other day. Emma has been asking questions about her, and today, I saw them talking. (*Pause, and no response from Hatrick.*) That Putnam fellow is an odd one. Sprawling here on the floor playing with Emma's toys. There's no way you're going to tell me that's a "normal" young man. (*Pause with no response.*)

HATRICK: Well, go on. Just get it all out of your system!

JENNY: Well, I still haven't recovered from that European friend of yours—always lurking about, asking silly questions, too.

HATRICK: What kind of questions?

JENNY: Questions about my family. Was I religious? What kind of education did I have? And before he left, Charles, he began asking questions about Emma, too. That man is spooky!

HATRICK: Look, Jenny. He's from another country. He's just interested in Americans and he's a very brilliant man.

JENNY: What makes him brilliant? Do you have to be strange to be brilliant? Is that how it works? Sometimes I think you prefer those unbalanced people to healthy ones! Since Marjorie's death and my moving in here, you've just seemed to turn off. You never leave this house—

HATRICK: Jesus Christ! (*Pause.*) I'm sorry. Jenny, you know I couldn't get along without you. You are invaluable to this household. Emma loves you very much—and I must admit, it was difficult for me to adjust to your joining us at first, but I have become quite fond of you myself. But this is my life and my work and I do not appreciate your meddling in my business.

JENNY: Charles—running this household has become my business, and I have to think of Emma.

HATRICK: (*Slips.*) You were thinking of yourself, too.

JENNY: (*Bitter.*) You know, Charles, you doctors do not have the answers to everything.

HATRICK: (*Rising, barely controlling his temper.*) There are occasions when we do Jenny.

JENNY: (*Hurt.*) Well, not on this occasion . . .

(*He exits; Jenny sits in the chair as lights come up on swing area.*)

Scene 2

(*Banton and Putnam have been strolling stage right. They settle into the swing. An awkward moment before she speaks.*)

BANTON: Do you realize you've shut up?

PUTNAM: What?

BANTON: You haven't been talking about work at all.

PUTNAM: I know. I'm losing my concentration at the clinic. I'm getting careless.

BANTON: How?

PUTNAM: My mind is wandering in all directions. Like today. I was walking down the—oh, forget it, this is ridiculous.

BANTON: Come on . . . what?

PUTNAM: I'm embarrassed.

BANTON: (*She grabs him.*) Just say it!

PUTNAM: (*Slightly frightened of her.*) I was walking through maternity and I saw this little auburn haired baby. All I could think about for the rest of the day was having a baby.

BANTON: And why does that embarrass you?

PUTNAM: Well, it never dawned on me that I could create a life. Do you think about . . . ?

BANTON: I suppose. Doesn't everyone think about that at one time or another?

PUTNAM: Not the people I spend time with! I'm so tired of analysing, prognosticating—putting everybody in little neat categories—

BANTON: So why did you become a psychiatrist?

PUTNAM: I don't know. It seemed interesting. I thought my mind was superior, and . . . well, I've never admitted this to anyone . . . but I can't stand the sight of blood. (*They both laugh.*)

BANTON: How did you get through medical school?

PUTNAM: Quickly!

BANTON: (*Laughs.*) You are funny, Sanford.

PUTNAM: I'm glad you appreciate my quick tongue. (*He realizes his mistake.*) Quick wit . . .

BANTON: Sandy. How were you in anatomy class?

PUTNAM: (*Panic.*) It wasn't one of my strongest subjects, if you know what I mean.

BANTON: I know what you mean.

PUTNAM: I know you know!

BANTON: There's no reason to be so nervous about all of that.

PUTNAM: Can you believe that I'm my age, a medical student, and I still don't know what I'm doing . . .

BANTON: As soon as you realize it has nothing to do with knowledge and everything to do with feeling you'll be just fine. Do you realize sometimes you even kiss competitively.

PUTNAM: I'm sorry.

BANTON: There's no need to be sorry. You've just been living so long up here . . . (*She touches his head*) and I think it's time you took a visit to your body for a while.

PUTNAM: I don't think I like my body.

BANTON: I do.

PUTNAM: (*Embarrassed.*) Oh God! I hate it when you make me have these conversations. No wonder I don't know what I'm doing anymore. I feel like such an idiot. What could you possibly see in me?

BANTON: (*Pause.*) Room for improvement? (*He gets annoyed and stands up. She goes to him.*) That was a joke. Will you just relax. Everything is going to turn out just fine.

PUTNAM: When? And for how long?

(*Banton turns to walk away. Putnam grabs her rather roughly. Then softens, and gives her a sensuous kiss. Lights fade and come back up in the parlor where Jenny is reading the paper.*)

Scene 3

(*Emma enters with crayons and paper and sits. There is a moment of silence. This conversation begins very casually—perhaps almost too casually.*)

JENNY: (*Not lifting her head from reading the paper.*) Did you have a good day at school?

EMMA: Uh huh.

JENNY: (*Pause.*) Rindy's mother telephoned today. She said she would bring you home from class tomorrow. (*No response.*)

EMMA: Okay.

JENNY: Will you look at this. Bertha Schneider is getting married! (*Mutters to herself in amazement. Reads.*) The Charity Ball will be held at the Coach House Inn . . . Mrs. Harry Kessler will chair the event . . . The society page is almost as discouraging as the front—(*Looks up and sees Emma.*) EMMA! I asked you not to crayon in the parlor! (*No response.*) Emma . . . do you *hear* me, young lady! (*Emma turns slowly to Jenny; Jenny is immediately alarmed.*) What's the matter? (*Goes to her.*)

EMMA: I just don't feel right.

JENNY: (*Pulls her up.*) You look pale, Emma. (*Touches her.*) My God, you're burning up! Why didn't you tell me you didn't feel well?

EMMA: I didn't want to have to go to bed.

JENNY: Tell me what hurts.

EMMA: Sometimes my head and chest.

JENNY: Sometimes! You mean you haven't been feeling well for a while?

EMMA: Uh huh. Usually it just goes away. But . . . (*Starts to cry*) . . . I felt awful in school today—all day, and now I don't feel right, either.

JENNY: (*Holds her warmly.*) That's okay, baby. You have to go to bed now. (*Begins to help her go upstairs.*) We'll get a doctor in to see you. (*Music.*)

EMMA: But Daddy's a doctor . . .

JENNY: He's not the right kind, Em. Now, you have to tell me when you're not feeling well. You mustn't be afraid . . .

[IX]

(*As Jenny and Emma disappear going up the stairs, Putnam appears in Emma's bedroom and Banton below it. Putnam takes what appears to be a bedsheet from the bed, and slowly drops the long silken cloth to Banton. As lights dim, Banton makes a wedding train out of the sheet and slowly marches up the stairs. Putnam meets her at the top, stretching the cloth from behind, creating a white wall behind which Emma, unseen by the audience, and now wearing a night gown, walks. They carry the cloth in front and around the bed, pulling it off-stage on their exit, revealing Emma lying still in the bed. Blackout.*)

Scene 4

(*Hatrick and Putnam are in the study. There is a noticeable change in their disposi-tions. Hatrick is preoccupied and distant. Putnam is uneasy. Rindy is seen walking to Emma's room.*)

HATRICK: Many people are rolling on an ant heap, being attacked by ants. The dreamer in a panic falls into a river.

PUTNAM: Did the dream establish a location for the dream . . . is it in a familiar place?

HATRICK: No. It's not really a specific place . . . somewhere in Europe.

PUTNAM: Well, how old is the dreamer? Is it a man or a woman?

HATRICK: Just tell me what you make of the dream!

PUTNAM: (*Annoyed.*) I would guess it was an older person, probably a woman, although that's simply intuition. Did this person identify any of the people in the dream?

HATRICK: No.

PUTNAM: Is this person suffering from some psychosis?

HATRICK: No.

PUTNAM: Well . . . it sounds to me like our mystery dreamer is either cracking up or at death's door. What the hell is this Charles? Twenty questions?

HATRICK: It's important for me to know what you can deduce from this in-formation.

PUTNAM: I don't know. There's not enough information. Go to a fortune teller or one of your mystic friends! Don't you see the absurdity of this conversation? Here we sit, with our brandy, all nicely dressed and comfy discussing a terrifying dream, someone's horror and pain. (*Pause.*)

HATRICK: What's going on?

PUTNAM: I don't know. I've lost my interest in all of this.

HATRICK: In what?

PUTNAM: In this profession. The business of twisted minds.

HATRICK: And what brought this on?

PUTNAM: I'm discovering other things . . .

HATRICK: Come on, come on—what other things?

PUTNAM: Day to day things . . .

HATRICK: What day to day things?

PUTNAM: I've taken up with a woman.

HATRICK: (*Amused.*) Ah hah. So that's it . . .

PUTNAM: It's nice, it's simple. I've never been with anyone before. Let's face it, the only thing I've ever known how to hold has been a book. I have not been familiar with "normal" if you know what I mean.

HATRICK: Tell me about normal—I'd love to know.

PUTNAM: Normal is not spending your days going on rounds with Dr. Winston.

HATRICK: He's up and about on two feet again?

PUTNAM: (*Not amused.*) Normal is not spending your days with a bunch of crazies in order to be certain of your own mental health.

HATRICK: I was sorry to hear about the patient you were treating. Her suicide has nothing to do with you.

PUTNAM: Wait a minute. There's no need to be sorry. In her place I would have done exactly the same thing. She would never be part of reality again, and I was just being naive to think that I could help her.

HATRICK: You did help her Sandy. Even Winston told me about your interest in her. You can't consider your efforts a failure and you can't deny feeling when you're dealing with patients.

PUTNAM: I know all of that. It's just that I want to help myself now. I've discovered an area I know nothing about and now I want to give in to that.

HATRICK: Well, that's hardly a profession.

PUTNAM: I know you think this is amusing, Charles. But I don't wish to spend my days in some private practice holding rich neurotic women's hands like you!

HATRICK: (*Impatient.*) Look Sandy, you are experiencing the most human of instincts, and if I may say so, you're finally growing up a little. There is a standard cliche, "Only the wounded physician heals."

PUTNAM: Oh, that's really brilliant!

HATRICK: (*Upset.*) Look, I go through periods of uncertainty, too. (*Pause.*) Emma's ill.

PUTNAM: (*Startled.*) What's the matter?

HATRICK: I don't wish to go into the details. I've been very . . . short-tempered.

PUTNAM: Is it serious?

HATRICK: I'm not certain.

PUTNAM: I'm sorry Charles. I'm very fond of Emma.

HATRICK: Thank you, Sanford . . . Don't be rash. It would be a terrible mistake for you to give up what you have learned.

PUTNAM: Charles, what I have learned will always be with me. And, I'm afraid I've already given my notice.

HATRICK: I know that, and it upset me that I had to learn about your decision from the clinic and not from you.

PUTNAM: I've been scared to tell you.

HATRICK: You can rethink your decision without penalty—I've seen to that.

PUTNAM: Thank you, but I cannot be entrusted with unstable lives when I am feeling so unfocused.

HATRICK: For crying out loud, what are you going to do?

PUTNAM: Well . . . I hear there's a great need for pathologists . . .

(*Hatrick freezes for a moment, then shaking his head goes over and puts his arm around Putnam.*)

Scene 5

(*Rindy is jumping up and down on Emma's bed in an attempt to get her up to play. Emma laughs at Rindy's antics until Rindy jumps from the bed and tries to pull her out.*)

EMMA: Rindy, don't.
RINDY: Come on. Get out of there.
EMMA: I'm sick and I have to stay in bed.
RINDY: You've been sick forever.
EMMA: I know.
RINDY: Aren't you tired of being sick?
EMMA: Yes. I wish I could go to Miss Banton's class.
RINDY: It's not so much fun without you. Guess what? I think Miss Banton has a boyfriend.
EMMA: Really?
RINDY: Uh huh! A real goony looking guy too. (*They giggle.*) What's it like to be sick?
EMMA: I'm sort of tired.
RINDY: You're not going to die, are you?
EMMA: Rindy! Jenny says if I rest enough I'll be able to be better real soon.
RINDY: Boy, I hate rest.

(*Rindy gets back on the bed and starts fooling around. Emma protests but Rindy ignores her and picks up a pillow and tries to instigate a fight. There are screams and giggles when Jenny dashes into the room.*)

JENNY: Get off that bed young lady.
RINDY: We were just having a pillow fight!
JENNY: Rindy, you know that Emma is sick and you were supposed to have a short, quiet visit.
EMMA: I'm tired of being sick.
RINDY: Yeah, me too.
JENNY: (*Touched.*) I know girls. I'll tell you what. How would you like me to read you a story? Would you like that?
RINDY *and* EMMA: Yeah!
JENNY: Okay. Emma, which book? (*Emma points to one. Jenny situates the girls*

on the bed.) Pick the story you want Emma. (*She does so.*) Okay. Everybody comfortable? (*Reads.*) "Once upon a time there lived a wise and honorable king who sat daily upon his throne dispensing favors and justice. Everyday for ten years a holy man in the dress of a beggar appeared and, without a word, presented the king with a gift of fruit. The royal king would accept the gift and pass it along without a thought to his treasurer. One day after the mendicant . . ."

RINDY: What's a mendicant?

JENNY: (*Miffed, but faking it.*) Emma, do you know what a mendicant is?

EMMA: It's just another name for a beggar.

JENNY: Right! . . . "so the beggar had presented his gift when a monkey appeared and bit into the fruit. When the animal bit it, a valuable jewel dropped out and rolled across the floor . . .

(*Hatrick enters the hallway and listens to the story outside the room.*)

"The king turned to the treasurer and asked: 'What has become of all the other gifts of fruit?' He replied, 'They have been thrown into the corner of the royal treasury!' And upon further investigation, to everyone's amazement, they found a pile of jewels amidst the rotting fruit.

"The king was astonished. 'Beggar, you have been generous to me without ever having asked for a favor. Now *I* must ask you to speak and tell me what I can do to repay these gifts.' The beggar replied: 'Oh, just King. There is a spirit that needs to be freed. Only you can perform that act of magic in the great burial ground. And so the next morning. . .'"

RINDY: Hello, Dr. Hatrick.

JENNY: Well, look who's here.

HATRICK: Well, hello ladies. (*Enters room.*)

EMMA: Hi, Papa.

HATRICK: How are you feeling Em?

EMMA: Okay.

HATRICK: Good. Rindy, bad news. Your Mom called and wants you home right away.

RINDY: The story was just getting good!

JENNY: Well, we'll finish another day, honey.

RINDY: Bye, Em. (*Rindy and Jenny exit from the bedroom.*)

EMMA: Bye, Rindy! . . . Daddy. How come I can't get out of bed? (*Hatrick sits next to her.*)

HATRICK: Well, you have to save your energy so you can get better.

EMMA: I do Daddy. I don't know what I'm doing wrong.

HATRICK: You're doing just fine, sweetie. You just have to be more patient.

EMMA: Would you scratch my back?

HATRICK: Sure. (*He does so.*) Emma, remember that book you gave me for Christmas.

EMMA: Uh huh.

HATRICK: What made you decide to give it to me?

EMMA: I'm not sure. You had so many books so I knew that you liked them, and so I made you one.

HATRICK: But, why a book of dreams?

EMMA: They were interesting stories, I guess.

HATRICK: And when did you have these dreams?

EMMA: When I was asleep.

HATRICK: (*Taken off guard.*) Of course, but—

EMMA: Did you like my book, Daddy?

HATRICK: Yes, Emma. Very much.

EMMA: Would you finish the story?

HATRICK: Certainly. Show me where. (*She does so.*) All right. (*Reads.*) ''The next morning, the king took his sword and met the beggar at the burial ground. The beggar said to the king: 'Go to the other end of the cemetery. You will find the corpse of a hanged man dangling from a tree. Your act of good will is to cut the corpse down and bring it to me.' '' (*Pauses in his reading.*) Are you sure you want to hear this?

EMMA: Sure. Why not?

HATRICK: (*Shakes his head.*) ''The king bravely crossed the howling ground until he came to a giant tree, where dangled the corpse of a man. The king climbed the tree and as he began to cut the body down it suddenly came to life, and said: 'Oh no you don't. You must answer each of my riddles in order to free this body.' Well, the king just ignored the remark and cut the body from the tree.

''But when the king climbed down to get the corpse, it flew back to the top. The king, amazed, climbed again to the top, where again the body came to life and told the king to answer each of his riddles before he would free the spirit.

''This time the king answered a riddle, but the answer was wrong and the corpse escaped the king's grasp. Over and over again this would happen until finally the king, exhausted, replied: 'I have no more answers for you! All of my royal knowledge is of no use. I don't have all of the answers to all of the riddles of the world.'

''And the spectre replied, 'You now understand the limitations of your earthly knowledge. Even a king such as you knows not everything. I am pleased by your bravery and determination. Now I will quit this spirit.' ''

(*Emma has fallen asleep but Hatrick continues.*)

"And so the king cut down the corpse and returned it to the beggar as he had promised. And just as one may discover on awakening that what has been obscure the day before is now understood, so the king came from his night of experience, full of wisdom and transformed."

[X]

(*Lights fade. Putnam, Banton, Rindy, Jenny and Professor stroll with picnic paraphernalia as if they were in a park. Music sets the tone for a sunny afternoon. They spread a blanket and all lie on it, chatting inaudibly.*)

(*Hatrick and Emma watch from the bedroom.*)

(*Suddenly, Rindy lets out a shriek and begins slapping herself as if something has bitten her. The group looks at her, seeing she is covered with ants. They begin slapping her, too, in an attempt to get them off. Their panic turns to themselves as they begin to be attacked. They howl and squirm feverishly on the ground, until they suddenly all stop, as if dead.*)

(*Emma comes down from her bedroom to the group. Hatrick comes down the steps with her but watches the proceedings from the foot of the stairs.*)

(*When Emma stoops down to Rindy, she is attacked too. She runs about in a frenzy screaming until she falls into a projection of water.*)

(*Silence.*)

(*Trowbridge enters with a roar of laughter surveying the debacle. She wears an enormous fur cape, dressed extravagantly. She pushes the bodies over with her feet, laughing endlessly. She then makes her way to the study where she passes Hatrick. He grabs her and they suddenly embrace in a long sensuous kiss. When they finish, Trowbridge steps away into the office. Hatrick is left holding the cape. Trowbridge is wearing an extraordinary scarlet red evening gown. Hatrick and Trowbridge freeze as everyone else exits.*)

Scene 6

(*Lights come up and we see Trowbridge feverishly pacing about the study. Hatrick, in a smoking jacket is noticeably on edge. At some point in this scene, we see Jenny on the second level helping the sick Emma into her bed.*)

TROWBRIDGE: Look at me. I'm shaking like a leaf.

HATRICK: Tell me what happened.

TROWBRIDGE: (*Near hysterical.*) My heart is pounding. I'm tingling all over.

HATRICK: Mrs. Trowbridge, collect yourself!

TROWBRIDGE: I didn't want to come here at this time of night . . .

HATRICK: It's quite all right. Now, please. Tell me what happened.

TROWBRIDGE: We were at the Charity Ball. I became very upset.

HATRICK: What do you mean?

TROWBRIDGE: It started about two nights ago . . .

HATRICK: Please sit.

TROWBRIDGE: (*She takes a deep breath and does so.*) It started two nights ago. I've never had problems with sleep. I always have a large glass of sherry before bedtime, then before I know it, it's morning. But two nights ago, I had the most dreadful dream.

HATRICK: Can you recall the dream?

TROWBRIDGE: I had this beautiful doll in my possession. It reminded me of dolls that I had as a child, though it was unlike any I had ever seen. Everyone wanted this doll, but I refused to relinquish it.

HATRICK: Who wanted it?

TROWBRIDGE: Well, first Mama or Papa came into our house—or was it their house? I can't remember . . . they were very angry, demanding that I hand over the doll. I said that I didn't know what they were talking about, but they said I did, and we then all ran off to my room—there you stood—and on my bed was, in fact this beautiful doll, which shocked me. I grabbed the doll as the three of you chased after me. I ran up the stairs to the attic and I heard Papa gasp from behind. As I turned to him, he grabbed his chest and fell back knocking Mama down and the stairs, and you as well. I woke up screaming—George had to hold me down, I was so hysterical.

HATRICK: Did the doll recall any particular image?

TROWBRIDGE: (*Nervous.*) Not really.

HATRICK: Was it a boy or a girl?

TROWBRIDGE: Girl.

HATRICK: And did you have the same dream the following night?

TROWBRIDGE: It was similar in that it revolved around the same object, but this time it was *I* who collapsed on the stairs as you wrested the child from my arms. Again I awoke in a panic. This morning I phoned Doctor Moore immediately and he sent a prescription.

HATRICK: And what happened this evening?

TROWBRIDGE: Well, I had been feeling fine all day. Just fine . . . So we went to the ball as planned. We were at our table. There were lots of gifts on the table—you know, door prizes, party favors and everyone began opening them, and when Harry Kessler opened his, it was a stuffed animal. Everyone thought it very amusing he would get such a prize and we burst out laughing and then I started to cry. My mind began to race back to the dream. It terrified me, that's all . . .

HATRICK: Have you any sense of what these dreams might mean?

TROWBRIDGE: Not really.

HATRICK: And the doll had no familiar appearance?

TROWBRIDGE: (*Troubled.*) Well . . .

HATRICK: Yes?

TROWBRIDGE: (*Pained.*) The doll, resembled your daughter. I didn't want to bring it up as I heard this evening that she was very ill.

HATRICK: I understand.

TROWBRIDGE: (*Realizing the truth.*) I am so sorry.

HATRICK: I appreciate that. When you were recalling the dream, you said that I wrested the "child" from your arms.

TROWBRIDGE: What?

HATRICK: You used the word "child" and not doll. (*She shakes her head 'no.'*) Have you ever wanted a child, Mrs. Trowbridge?

TROWBRIDGE: (*Getting up.*) George always said "If God intended us to have children, he would have sent us one."

HATRICK: But would you like to have had one?

TROWBRIDGE: (*Shrinking.*) Yes. I suppose. (*Aggravated.*) I must go now.

HATRICK: Have you ever gone to a doctor to see if you could conceive a child?

TROWBRIDGE: I can't.

HATRICK: How do you know that?

TROWBRIDGE: I know. I can't. I hurt myself, a long time ago.

HATRICK: How did you hurt yourself?

TROWBRIDGE: I was in love . . . I don't want to talk about this anymore . . . I'm frightened . . . (*Starts to run out, he restrains her.*)

HATRICK: Do you want to go on suffering these dreams and attacks?

TROWBRIDGE: (*In great pain.*) No!

HATRICK: Were you in love with the young man who worked for your father?

TROWBRIDGE: (*Stunned.*) Who?

HATRICK: You spoke once of a young man who worked for your father . . .

TROWBRIDGE: Oh . . .

HATRICK: Can you describe him?

TROWBRIDGE: (*She begins speaking in the voice of a child.*) He was the most beautiful man I have ever seen. Blonde. Tall. I wasn't a pretty little girl. I was awkward. They never let me dress my age. I was kept a child. Boys never paid attention to me. I never even understood such matters.

HATRICK: (*Letting go of her.*) Yes. Go on.

TROWBRIDGE: William came to the house one day—to bring something from the factory. I had just come out of the bath. I was wearing a cotton robe—nothing else. My hair was down. I heard the car and went to the window. There he was. I just stared at him from the window. He later told me the sunlight flooded in so—in through my gown, that he could see me beneath the cotton. We smiled at one another, then he drove off.

HATRICK: Then what? (*Hatrick retreats to his chair; Trowbridge moves center stage in front of him.*)

TROWBRIDGE: That night, I happened to look out my window, and I saw him standing across the street. Night after night, the same. Finally, one evening, Mama and Papa went out. The servants were in their quarters, and I crept out.

HATRICK: And what happened?

TROWBRIDGE: It just seemed so normal. Our bodies took control and everything seemed so wonderful . . . for a while.

HATRICK: Go on.

TROWBRIDGE: Then my body began to change. I was so stupid. I didn't even understand. I thought it was a part of nature. Growing up. It was nature all right. Sickness in the morning. Mama heard me ill one day and insisted that I see a doctor.

HATRICK: Finish the story.

TROWBRIDGE: (*Dropping back into adult voice; bitter.*) Mama fell to pieces. Mama couldn't cope. Papa became a crazed man. I was forbidden to leave the house. At night, I would look out my window and see William across the street. One day I tried to get a note to him, but father caught me. My world just stopped. I never had the chance to explain. I never saw him again. I knew I wouldn't.

HATRICK: What of the child?

TROWBRIDGE: (*Falling apart.*) Elaborate plans were made to send me away. The deception was carried to great lengths. All I could think of was him. There was a terrible row. Mama, Papa and me, all screaming at each other in the library. I completely lost control. God, I hated them! I hated myself even more. (*Cold, distant.*) I ran to my room and locked myself in, and with my fist . . . I began to beat myself. I pounded my stomach with all the force I could.

[XI]

(*Music. She slowly crosses through to the parlor.*) Yes. I beat myself until . . . How could they have done that to me. How could I have done that to myself. . . .

(*Trowbridge slowly staggers up the stairs towards Emma's room as she continues murmuring her story. Behind the scrim we see a man [Putnam] in a trench coat and hat with a stocking over his face, crossing towards the bedroom as well. Trowbridge gets to Emma and coaxes the child from the bed, and begins to lead her from the room. Emma carries the scarf she got from Trowbridge. The back wall to Emma's room opens and the man appears.)*

(Frightened, Trowbridge picks Emma up and leads her across the hallway and down the stairs. Putnam slowly follows them.)

(Hatrick remains seated. As Trowbridge crosses above, the bookcase in the study tracks off-stage revealing Jenny in the darkness behind. She is wearing a wedding veil and carrying a white luminous ball. She walks slowly towards the center of the parlor.)

(Emma clings to Trowbridge as they reach the center of the parlor. Trowbridge hugs Emma. Emma wraps the scarf around Trowbridge, then Trowbridge leaves Emma standing alone in the center of the room. Jenny proceeds forward, bends to allow Emma to touch the ball. As she touches it, the ball pops with a loud bang and vapors emanate from it. Putnam rushes from behind grabbing Emma who screams as she is carried from the room and the lights blackout.)

Scene 7

(Hatrick is in the study. He reads a letter. Professor has now moved back to the position from which his opening lecture was delivered.)

PROFESSOR: Charles. My journey back home was a safe, if somewhat bumpy affair. My brief stop in London, where I delivered a paper on alchemy, seemed to go well, though I admit, I have become uncertain of how my ideas are truly being met.

I wish to thank you again for your hospitality on my visit as well as your recent letter. I apologize for being so late in offering this expression of gratitude. Many thoughts have come forth since our short visit and I am sorry to have to continue our dialogue in this form.

(Jenny crosses the hallway carrying Emma. She puts the child in bed, then exits.)

Your news of Emma's illness came as a great shock. I am so very sorry. Of course our discussion of her dreams adds an eerie light to this dark news. Those dreams have returned to me with an unrelenting determination. I can only hope that this illness will be detoured from its seemingly inevitable course. The manner in which I discussed those dreams with you proves now to be something of an embarrassment. For one who is so quick to talk of the importance of feelings, in retrospect, my own fascination must have appeared heartless.

Charles, the separation from a loved one is a silence that cannot be touched. Perhaps I never expressed my sincere condolence at Marjorie's untimely death, so as poor Emma's life now weighs in the balance, please know that I am with you. Furthermore, Charles, I hope you can allow your own feelings to be adequately expressed. I recall your saying once, shortly after your wife's death, that you wished you could feel less. Unfortunately, to do so is simply to bury the moment, the result of which is another kind of death as well. My thoughts and affection are most certainly with you and Emma.

(*Rindy enters and goes to the door with a gift for Emma. Jenny comes to the door and takes the gift and heads up to Emma's room. Rindy, however remains, after the door is closed and sits on the doorstep.*)

JENNY: Emma, look. Rindy brought you a gift from her and Miss Banton. (*Jenny unwraps it slowly. It is a music box. Emma opens it and a lovely tune begins to play.*) Isn't that beautiful? You must be hungry. I'll go and bring you up your lunch.

(*As Jenny leaves, the scrim lights come up and we see Banton repeating her ballerina dance to the music. Slowly, Emma rises from her bed and with the music box in hand, makes her way slowly down the steps to the parlor.*)

PROFESSOR: Emma, I love that marvelous bird book you got for Christmas. And that bird record . . . Oh, that bird record.
TROWBRIDGE: (*Entering and sitting on the swing.*) Come give me a kiss, Emma. You are such a beautiful little girl. Come over here and give me a kiss.
PUTNAM: (*Enters on second level.*) You see, Emma, people tell me their dreams and I tell them what they mean. But, sometimes I can't tell.
BANTON: (*Joins Putnam.*) Are you coming to dance class today Emma? Do you have your dance clothes too?
JENNY: (*Enters and stands in back of parlor.*) It's time to wake up, Emma. It's a lovely day outside. It's time to wake up and get dressed.

(*Emma puts the music box down and stands in a pool of light. Hatrick approaches her from behind.*)

[XII]

HATRICK: Once upon a time, swarms of gnats covered up the sun, the moon and all of the stars in the sky, except one. That one star fell from the sky and landed on a pretty little dreamer.

(Emma falls back into her father's arms, and he carries her off-stage. Everyone else exits, except Rindy. The music box continues to play as Rindy slowly steps into the house and sneaks up to the music box. She shuts it. The music stops. Rindy looks up and sees the audience. Surprised, she takes the music box and dashes back out of the house as the lights fade to black.)

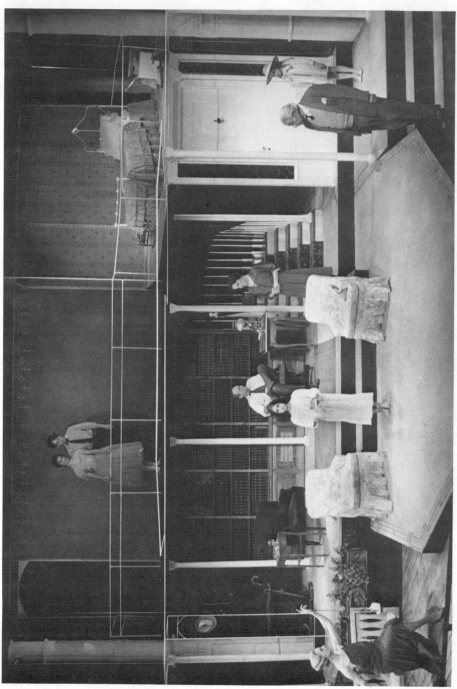